The Policeman Who Had Small Feet

Frank Flynn

Illustrated by
Tim Archbold

Paul Purves was a police constable. P.C. Paul was feared by robbers all over the world. He was clever, speedy and strong. He could think faster than a computer.

He could run quicker than a cheetah.

He could even pull a double-decker bus using just his teeth.

There was no doubt about it. P.C. Paul was the cleverest, fastest, strongest policeman around.

Only one thing worried P.C. Paul: his feet. For some reason, while the rest of his body had grown and grown, his feet had hardly increased in size at all. In fact, they had remained quite tiny.

Every morning P.C. Paul would line up with the other police constables for parade. He was the smartest P.C. in the line. His shoes were so highly polished that the Chief of Police had to wear sunglasses to inspect them. But all the other P.C.s giggled at Paul's small feet. Because they all had large feet, P.C. Paul was the odd one out.

Even the Chief of Police laughed at Paul's feet.

"Well, P.C. Paul," he would say, "not only are you the smartest, fastest, strongest man on the force, but you've also got the strangest feet I've ever seen."

And then he would laugh so much that his false teeth would fall out onto the floor, where they would carry on laughing by themselves.

HEE
HEE

P.C. Paul couldn't see the joke. He didn't think that his feet were funny. It made him feel very sad when everyone laughed at his feet. As far as he was concerned, they were good, strong feet.

Unfortunately, however, people kept laughing at Paul's feet and, in time, he came to believe that there really was something wrong with them. Feeling very gloomy he went for a long walk.

P.C. Paul walked up mountains and down valleys. He walked through towns with busy streets and through lonely country places. He did so much walking that he thought he was going to wear his small feet out. Try as he might, he couldn't come up with any good ideas for making his feet bigger.

Exhausted by all of this thinking and walking, Paul went into a cafe. He sat by the window, took off his hat, scratched his head and wondered what to do.

Paul ordered a mug of tea and some of his favourite ginger biscuits. Gazing out of the window, he stared at the feet of the people who passed by. He saw feet with black shoes and feet with brown shoes; feet with yellow wellingtons and feet with shiny red boots.

Suddenly P.C. Paul jumped up,
scratched his nose, and said "That's it! I
know just what to do."

So he put on his hat and did just that.

Off he went to the nearest shoe shop
to buy the biggest pair of boots that he
could find. The boots he chose were big
enough to fit a giant.

But boots big enough to fit a giant are very heavy boots. These were so heavy that P.C. Paul could hardly lift his feet. When he tried to chase robbers over fences or down streets, he kept tripping over his own boots and falling over.

Once, when he was chasing a burglar across a muddy building site, one of Paul's boots got tangled up with his other boot. He fell PLOP on his face in the middle of a large puddle.

Sitting up surrounded by diggers, dumpers and steamrollers, P.C. Paul took off his hat and scratched his head. He decided that the huge boots were a bad idea. He looked around and tried to think of another way to make his feet bigger.

Suddenly he jumped up, scratched his nose and said, "That's it! I know just what to do."

So he put on his hat and did just that.

The next day P.C. Paul was on traffic duty in the middle of the High Street. He directed cars one way and lorries the other.

He helped old ladies and children across the busy street.

He kept the traffic moving and the people safe. Finally he saw what he had been waiting for: a large yellow steamroller was coming along the street towards him.

The big yellow machine rumbled and clanked on its heavy rollers. As it drew near to P.C. Paul, he stuck his feet directly in its path. Without giving even a little bump, the yellow machine passed over P.C. Paul's feet. The steamroller squashed Paul's feet as flat as a pair of kippers.

When he looked down at his newly flattened feet, P.C. Paul felt pleased. They looked much bigger than they had before.

But when he tried to walk, he found
that he could only waddle like a large
penguin. Everyone in the street laughed
at him. Drivers stopped their cars to point
at the policeman who waddled down the
street like the tallest penguin in the world.

For the rest of that week, P.C. Paul had
to wear a special pair of flipper-shaped
slippers until his feet shrank back to their
normal size.

With a mug of cocoa and a plate of ginger biscuits, P.C. Paul sat down in front of his TV set and wondered what to do.

While he was staring at the screen, an advertisement for a trip around the world flashed in front of his eyes and a voice said, "Travel around the world. Find what you are looking for."

P.C. Paul jumped out of his seat,
spilling his cocoa as he did so. He said,
"That's it! I know just what to do."
So he put on his hat and did just that.

P.C. Paul walked all the way to India. He tramped along straight, flat roads. He tramped up high roads that snaked their way over snow-covered mountains. He searched and searched for someone who might be able to help him to make his feet grow. Finally, he met a man called a yogi who had special magical powers.

The yogi taught P.C. Paul how to walk across red-hot coals without burning the soles of his feet.

He taught P.C. Paul how to dance through flames without toasting his toes.

He even showed Paul how to bend his body this way and that, without breaking any bones.

But despite being able to show P.C. Paul how to bend himself backward like a rubber bridge, the yogi was unable to teach Paul how to make his feet grow.

Wondering what he should do next, P.C. Paul sat down on the hot coals, took off his hat, scratched his head and thought. Absent-mindedly he picked up a stick shaped like a boomerang and flung it into the air. Whizzing in a curve, it promptly came back and hit P.C. Paul on the head.

After rubbing the lump that appeared where the boomerang struck, P.C. Paul smiled a big smile, scratched his nose and said, "That's it! I know just where to go next."

So he put on his hat and did just that.

P.C. Paul sailed to Australia on a great
big ship.

"Kangaroos seem to have pretty big
feet," he said. "Maybe they will know
how I can make my feet grow."

The kangaroos were a friendly bunch.
They taught P.C. Paul how to hop without
ever needing to stop. They hopped across
deserts and they hopped through fields.
They hopped across mountains and they
hopped through streams. But after all of
the hopping was over, they couldn't show
P.C. Paul how to make his feet grow.

Feeling just a little sad, P.C. Paul sat down in the shade of a eucalyptus tree. He took off his hat, scratched his head and wondered what he could do about his tiny feet. Just then, a koala bear climbed out of the tree and sat on P.C. Paul's head.

P.C. Paul smiled, tickled the bear's
tummy, scratched his own nose and said,
"That's it! I know what to do next."
So he put on his hat and did just that.

P.C. Paul jumped into a plane and flew
all the way to the North Pole. He
parachuted down into the soft, deep snow.

When he stood up, he looked like a
police snowman.

A bewildered but helpful polar bear taught P.C. Paul how to walk on ice without any shoes. But Paul didn't think that was very nice. As he walked through the snow and the ice, he shivered and shook. He became so cold that he started to turn blue.

After sliding around on the ice for a week and a day, P.C. Paul realised that the shaggy old bear would not be able to show him how to make his feet grow.

With snow falling around, P.C. Paul sat down, took off his hat, scratched his head and wondered what he should do next.

He sat all day and most of the night. Staring at the smiling face of the full moon, he saw a shooting star zoom across the sky.

P.C. Paul smiled back at the moon, scratched his nose and said, "That's it! I know just where to go next."

So he put on his hat and did just that.

He went to America where he trained
as an astronaut, and then caught a rocket
to outer space.

When he arrived in that weightless
place, he floated around until he met
some aliens. They had small green bodies
with ten long legs and ... ten huge feet!

"At last!" P.C. Paul said to himself.
Surely these aliens, with ten enormous
feet each, would know how to help him
to make his feet grow.

43

So Paul willingly let them take him to
a strange purple planet with three red
moons. The aliens showed him some
wonderful things. They showed him how
to walk on air

and how to ride a shooting star

and how to drink while upside down. But
what they didn't and couldn't show P.C.
Paul, was how to make his feet grow.

45

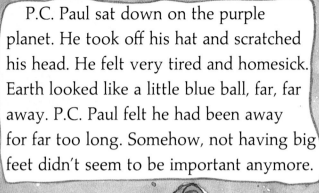

P.C. Paul sat down on the purple planet. He took off his hat and scratched his head. He felt very tired and homesick. Earth looked like a little blue ball, far, far away. P.C. Paul felt he had been away for far too long. Somehow, not having big feet didn't seem to be important anymore.

P.C. Paul smiled at his thought, scratched his nose and said, "That's it! I'm going home."

So he put on his hat and did just that.

Safely back home, sipping a cup of cocoa and nibbling a ginger biscuit, P.C. Paul stared at his feet and said, "My feet might not be very big, but they are the only ones I've got. From now on, I'm going to be satisfied with them just the way they are."

And P.C. Paul never wished for a bigger pair of feet from that day forward.